I wish!

Bel Mooney

illustrated by Margaret Chamberlain

EGMONT

For Bryony Jade Ball
who wishes the whole world
could be green

First published in Great Britain 1995
by Methuen Children's Books Limited

This edition published 2003 by Egmont Books Limited,
239 Kensington High Street, London W8 6SA

Text copyright © 1995 Bel Mooney
Illustrations copyright © 1995 Margaret Chamberlain

ISBN 1 4052 0382 X

5 7 9 0 8 6

A CIP catalogue record for this title
is available from the British Library

Printed in Great Britain
by Cox & Wyman Ltd, Reading, Berkshire

Contents

There are 12 brilliant titles in the
Kitty and **friends** series.
Collect them all!

I don't want to!
I can't find it!
It's not fair!
But you promised!
Why not?
I know!
I'm scared!
I wish!
Why me?
I'm bored!
It's not my fault!
So what!

I wish!

...it was mine!

It was the day after William's birthday, and for the first time in her life Kitty felt jealous of her friend next door.

Very jealous.

Horribly jealous.

So jealous she started to wish all sorts of bad things – like William would fall over and hurt his leg. That was because she knew if something like that happened he wouldn't be able to use his wonderful present.

1

William had got a new bike for his birthday, and Kitty wanted one more than anything else in the world. It was a fast, sporty green bike with lots of gears.

Kitty had grown out of her old red bike, and wished hard for a new one. 'Can I get a bike like that for my birthday, Mum?' asked Kitty.

Kitty's mum shook her head. 'I don't think so, love. We couldn't afford it right now. We could maybe look for a second-hand bike . . .'

Kitty stamped her foot. 'I don't want a silly old second-hand bike. I want a new bike, just like William's.'

'Well, you can't have one,' said her mother, sounding cross, but sad at the same time.

Now Kitty knew the reason. Just two months ago, her dad had lost his job, and so Mum said they all had to be careful with money until he found a new one. But

I wish!

although Kitty tried to remember Dad's kind, worried face, and be good – she kept thinking of William's bike.

'I wish it was mine – oh, I *wish* it was mine,' she said to herself, over and over again.

Out of the window she watched William riding his bike up and down the road.

'He's so mean – he hasn't even asked me if I want a go,' she muttered to herself.

But when William came to the door and asked just that, Kitty said, 'No, I've got some homework to do,' in a sulky voice, and closed the door in his face.

That night Kitty couldn't sleep. She kept on thinking about the bike, and wishing it was hers, and tossing and turning – and feeling very unhappy.

The next day it was worse. Dad went out, and came back with a big grin on his face. 'Come outside, Kit,' he shouted, 'we've got a surprise for you!'

I wish!

Kitty went to the back door to see Dad standing proudly – by a bike. 'Your Auntie Susan said you could have Melissa's old bike,' said Dad. 'Isn't that great?'

Kitty looked at the bike. It had a little basket on the front, and it was pink. PINK! She didn't know what to say – because she didn't want to hurt Dad's feelings.

'Do you like it?' he asked.

'Er . . . yes,' she said, in a small voice.

'You don't sound very pleased,' said Dad.

Kitty found she wanted to cry.

'Go on, Kitty,' said Mum, coming out of the kitchen. 'Take it out on the pavement – I think William's still there. But be careful!'

'I don't want to . . . not now,' gulped Kitty. She couldn't bear to think of the other children laughing at the old *girly* bike.

'Oh,' said Dad. He sounded really disappointed, which made Kitty feel worse than ever.

Just then William put his head through the hole in the fence. 'Hallo!' he said. 'Do you want to come out and play, Kit?'

Kitty stood in front of the awful pink bike, so he wouldn't see it. But she was too late.

'What's that?' he asked, coming through.

'We've got Melissa's old bike for Kit

I wish!

– so now she can go for a ride with you,' said Kitty's dad.

William looked at Kitty, then at her dad, and then at the bike.

'I'm not going out,' mumbled Kitty, going bright red.

'Why not?' said William. 'I'll tell you what, you can ride my bike, and I'll ride yours. Then we'll swap.'

Kitty couldn't believe her ears. She stared at William. Dad looked really pleased, and went inside.

'You want to ride this bike?' asked Kitty.

'Yes – we can carry a couple of cans of drink in the basket. And some crisps,' said William.

'William, I . . . I don't like it,' whispered Kitty.

'I know,' said William.

'I wish I had a bike like yours,' whispered Kitty.

'Shhh – I know,' said William. 'That's

why you can ride it whenever you like.'

'You really don't mind riding this old thing?' asked Kitty.

William shook his head. 'Bet I make it go just as fast as mine,' he grinned.

Kitty looked at her friend. 'You know something? I wish I was as nice as you, William,' she said.

William stuck out his tongue at her and ran away. 'Now you really *are* wishing for the moon, Kit!' he said.

I wish!

...he'd go away!

Daniel was being really horrible to Kitty. She knew that big brothers are usually a *bit* horrid – that's what being a big brother is all about!

But for a week now he had been worse than ever. He argued with Kitty about what to watch on television. When Kitty asked him to play cards he said no. When Kitty broke Mum's vase and tried to glue it together again, he told on her.

To make it worse, he was grumpy and grouchy the whole time, and nobody could make him smile. Not even Mum.

Kitty decided he was the worst brother in the whole world.

'I hate Daniel,' she said to Mum.

'No, you don't, dear,' said Mum.

'But I do! I think he's horrid and I wish he'd go away!' shouted Kitty.

'You'd miss him then!' smiled Mum.

'No, I wouldn't! I wish he would go away, and then I'd be happy!' said Kitty, tossing her head.

I wish!

She jumped up from the chair – and knocked over the little table with the lamp on it. The lamp fell on the ground, and the shade came rolling off. When Kitty went to pick it up she got her foot caught in the wire – and fell over. Just then Dan came in, saw what a mess she had made – and started to laugh. He laughed and laughed – and Mum joined in.

'Go away! GO AWAY!' screamed Kitty.

The next day, Kitty had to get to school early because her class was going on a trip. She sat next to Rosie on the coach,

and enjoyed the visit to the old castle. On the way back they played word games and sang some songs, and had such fun that Kitty forgot her bad mood. She was looking forward to telling Mum all about her day.

But when the coach got back to the school gates, she saw that Mum looked worried.

'Oh Kitty – guess what? Poor Dan's in hospital. He had bad pains in his tummy – and they think it might be his appendix.'

'What's a pendix?' asked Kitty.

'Oh, it's a funny little thing inside us that can hurt,' said Mum.

They went home, and Kitty was left with William while Mum and Dad went to see Daniel. When they came home at last, they told her Daniel would have to stay in hospital for two or three days.

That night the house seemed very empty, with just the three of them. Mum and Dad tried to be cheerful, but Kitty could tell they were worried.

I wish!

The next night it was the same. Kitty tried to tell them jokes, but they didn't laugh. At last she went to bed – first looking into her brother's empty room.

She was in bed when she heard the telephone ring, then lots of talking, then silence. Kitty felt very unhappy. She decided that she was 'a pendix' too – because she was a funny little thing that hurt inside.

When Mum came up to say goodnight, Kitty was very quiet. She clutched Mr Tubs as if somebody was going to take him away – then burst into tears.

'What's the matter, Kit?' asked Mum.

'It's . . . it's . . . it's *my fault*,' sobbed Kitty.

'What's your fault, love?'

'Daniel . . .'

'Oh, don't be silly!' smiled Mum.

'But . . . but . . . *I wished he would go away, and now he has gone away*. So it's all my fault!'

Mum gave Kitty a big hug. 'Do you think wishes come true as easily as that, Kit?' she asked. Kitty sniffed and nodded.

Mum gave a little laugh. 'Why, then it would be too easy to hurt people, wouldn't it? We all sometimes wish for bad things to happen. But it's not our fault if they do – do you hear me, pet?'

Kitty nodded.

'I wish Dan would come back,' she said.

'That's one wish that WILL come true,' said Mum, 'because the hospital's just rung to say we can bring him home tomorrow!'

I wish!

. . . I was pretty!

'Oh no!' groaned Daniel.

'Save us!' said Kitty.

'I'll hide!' snapped Daniel.

'I'll run away!' growled Kitty.

'She's so *boring*!' they yelled, both together.

Only one thing made the children agree like that. Mum had just told them cousin Melissa was coming to stay for a night.

'It's all right for you, Dan – you don't have to play with her,' said Kitty.

'Phew!' grinned Daniel.

Melissa arrived with a big suitcase, which she dropped with a crash on Kitty's bedroom floor. The camp bed was already up, but Melissa looked at it and frowned.

'I don't want to sleep on *that* old thing,' she said. 'Last time it made my back sore.'

Kitty's mum heard, and patted Melissa's head. 'Don't worry, dear, Kitty will give you her bed, won't you Kitty?'

'Thanks, Mum,' said Kitty, in a cross voice.

I wish!

That was the trouble with Melissa. Everybody fussed over her. It made Kitty *so* mad!

She watched Melissa unpack her things. For one night she seemed to have brought an awful lot. She was already wearing a really smart little kilt with a cream jumper – which Kitty would have thought too posh even for best.

'What's that dress for?' asked Kitty, as Melissa hung it in the wardrobe.

'Oh, I thought I might like to look pretty for supper,' said Melissa.

'What for?' asked Kitty sitting on the floor.

'Because it's nice to look pretty,' said Melissa. Then she looked at Kitty as if she was something off another planet.

'Oh, but you wouldn't care, would you?' she said.

'No, I jolly well wouldn't!' said Kitty – picking at a large lump of mud that was stuck to the bottom of her jeans.

A bit later, William came round. After a while Kitty noticed something strange. Melissa was being SO nice to William it was like she had been dipped in sugar. Worse – William was being nice back.

Too nice.

It wasn't natural.

He gave Melissa his last sweet. He

listened politely when she went on and on about some new girl in her class. When they started to play *Frustration*, he let her have his go, because she was losing. *And* he jumped up to get the die when she threw too hard and it rolled across the floor.

When Kitty won, and Melissa made a face, he said, 'Don't worry, Melissa, it's only luck, not skill.'

'Thanks a lot!' said Kitty.

As he was leaving to go home, William looked at Melissa and said, in a funny shy voice, 'I like that skirt-thing. You look really nice.'

It was then that Kitty felt a bit sick.

That night, when the girls were getting ready for bed, Melissa washed her face carefully, and brushed her hair so that it stood all round her head like a golden crown. She put on a pretty pink nightie, and smiled at herself in the mirror.

Kitty wore an old T-shirt for bed, and her hair was its usual tangle. Melissa looked at her and laughed. 'Oh, Kitty, we look like Beauty and the Beast. Or the Princess and the Pea. And you're the pea . . . !' She collapsed in giggles. 'Oh, thanks!' scowled Kitty.

Kitty was very quiet next morning. Melissa just wanted to watch television. Kitty kept looking at her, and thinking

I wish!

how silly she was – and how much she wished her cousin would go home.

At last Auntie Susan arrived in a rush – and Kitty had her wish.

She went upstairs to her bedroom, and stood for a long time looking in the mirror. She hadn't washed her face, and her hair was tangled, and she was wearing her old jeans and T-shirt.

The wardrobe door was open. Kitty noticed that Melissa had forgotten the smart dress. She looked at it – then back at herself in the mirror. And she had an idea.

Kitty and friends

Mum and Dad were talking in the kitchen, and Dan was sitting at the table – when the door opened.

'Good heavens . . .!' said Dad.

'Kitty, what have you done to yourself?' gasped Mum.

'Oh . . . oh . . . you look . . . so *funny*,' choked Daniel.

Kitty had washed and brushed her hair, and tied it back into neat bunches. Her face was clean. And she was wearing Melissa's blue dress – with a white collar and cuffs. Mum and Dad and Daniel roared with laughter.

'Stop laughing!' Kitty yelled, stamping her foot. Then she ran from the room.

Dad ran after her – and found her in the sitting-room. She was lying on the settee, with her head under a cushion. 'Oh, Kitty-Kat – what are you up to? Why did you dress yourself up like that?'

A muffled voice said, 'I wish I was pretty.'

'Oh,' said Dad, 'so *that's* it. Come here . . .'

He sat Kitty on his knee, and said, 'But Mum and I think you *are* pretty, Kit! Not that it matters anyway – we like you just the way you are.'

'But people like the way Melissa looks,' muttered Kitty. 'So I wish . . .'

'DON'T say you wish you looked like Melissa,' grinned Dad, 'cos I couldn't stand that!'

'Nor could I,' said Mum, coming in.

'Nor me!' said Daniel, standing next to her.

Kitty looked up at them all, and saw they meant it. Then she looked down and started to laugh.

'I'll tell you something, Kit,' said Mum. 'I WISH you'd take that awful dress off and get back into your scruffy clothes.'

And of course, that wish came true in a moment!

I wish!

...you'd shut up!

It wasn't as much fun in school as usual, because everybody seemed to be quarrelling. First Anita fell out with Rosie and said she didn't want to be her friend any more.

Then, because Kitty was going round with Anita, Rosie got hurt, and Kitty felt caught in the middle. Then Rosie and Anita made up, and Kitty felt left out. So she started hanging round William. But

Kitty and friends

William wasn't so friendly in school, because he liked being with big Tom, who said he didn't like girls . . .

So it was all very silly, and a bit messy. Kitty thought she should do something about it.

She went up to Anita and Rosie in the playground and said, 'Hallo.'

I wish!

'Anybody would think we hadn't seen you today,' said Rosie.

Kitty decided to take no notice. She looked at the scarf Anita had just thrown over her head and, because she wanted to please her friend, said, 'I like that colour.'

'It's only blue,' said Anita.

'Yes, but it's a *nice* blue,' said Kitty.

Anita shrugged and said nothing. So Kitty tried again. 'I heard a good joke the other day,' she said. 'What's green and red and . . .'

'Oh, Kitty, *I WISH YOU'D SHUT UP!*' said Rosie.

Kitty stopped, with her mouth open. Then she closed her mouth, looked at her friends – and wanted to cry. But instead, in a very quiet voice, she said, 'Wishes can come true, Rosie.' Then she walked away.

Kitty decided she would do just what Rosie said, and not speak at all. That would show them! The trouble was, if she decided not to speak to her friends, she would have to be really brave and not speak to the teacher either.

It was history, Kitty's favourite subject, and they were learning about the Romans.

'Kitty! Stand up and tell us what the Roman soldiers wore,' said Miss Smith.

Kitty shook her head.

'Don't you know? You drew such a lovely picture . . .'

Kitty nodded her head like a puppet.

'Then speak!'

Kitty shook her head.

The children started to giggle. Miss Smith frowned and said, 'Now, don't be so silly, Kitty.'

Kitty shook her head from side to side.

More children laughed. Kitty was determined not to give in. 'Come out here!' said Miss Smith sternly.

Kitty walked to the front of the class, and stood by the blackboard. 'Now what

have you got to say for yourself?' asked
Miss Smith.

Turning to the blackboard, Kitty wrote
a figure 'O'.

The children laughed and laughed, but
Miss Smith went bright red. 'Stop playing

this silly trick at once, Kitty,' she said – in a very loud voice.

Kitty knew she had to explain, but she was determined not to speak. So she went to the teacher's desk, and wrote quickly on a piece of paper. Miss Smith read it: 'Somebody said they wished I would shut up, so now I have.'

'I see,' said the teacher, looking closely at Kitty, and seeing she was upset. 'So who told you to shut up then?'

Kitty shook her head.

'Whoever it was is *very* rude. I don't like nasty, rude children in my class. Now go and sit down, Kitty.'

Kitty didn't look at Rosie, as she went back to her table. Rosie ducked her head down anyway, hiding her face.

At lunchtime lots of children crowded round Kitty, trying to make her speak. It was a great game, and everybody seemed in a good mood. But it was no good. She

stayed quiet. 'You're really good at this, Kit!' said William.

Only Rosie and Anita didn't come near, and that made Kitty sad. I'll jolly well stay shut up until Rosie undoes her wish! she said to herself.

In the afternoon, Miss Smith kept looking at Kitty. Usually Kitty talked a lot. Miss Smith didn't like to see her

looking so silent and sad. So she clapped
her hands and said, 'Children, I'm going
to give a prize to the person who can make
Kitty speak!'

The children were excited. 'But how do
we do that, Miss?' someone called.

'Only one person can make Kitty speak,
and get the prize,' said Miss Smith, 'and
that's the person who told her to shut up.
Say that person was a wicked witch who
put a bad spell on Kitty, now she has to be
a good witch and take the spell off. If it is
a "she", of course?'

She looked around the class. All the
children looked at each other, but some of
them looked at Rosie – because they knew.
At last Rosie put up her hand, looking
very ashamed.

'I can make Kitty speak, Miss Smith,'
she said.

'Go on then!' said Miss Smith with
a smile.

'Kitty – I'm sorry, and I wish you'd speak to us again,' said Rosie.

Kitty felt her face go pink, as she said, 'All right.' But the words came out in such a funny squeak – like a rusty old door that hasn't been opened for a long time. Kitty coughed and started to laugh.

Rosie laughed too, and so did Anita, and Miss Smith, and all the children. It was a lovely, warm, happy sound.

'What's Rosie's prize, Miss?' Tom called out.

'What do you think it is, Rosie?' asked Miss Smith.

And Rosie said, 'It's Kitty being noisy again!'

I wish!

... wishes came true!

Kitty was reading a fairy tale about an old couple who were given three wishes. They quarrelled, and wished for silly things – like a sausage. And then their life went on as before, when they had nothing.

She closed the book with a sigh. What a waste of good luck! Fancy having three wishes and not wishing for wonderful things . . .

Just then, Daniel came into the sitting-

room, carrying some school books. He sat down at the table and groaned.

'Oh, I *wish* they didn't give us so much homework,' he said.

'Now if you had a real wish, and you wished for that it would waste the wish,' said Kitty.

'You wouldn't say that if you had all this work to do!' grinned Dan.

'What would you wish for, if you had three wishes, and you knew they would come true?' asked Kitty.

'That's easy! You wouldn't want three

I wish!

– you'd just need one wish.'

'Why?' asked Kitty.

'You'd wish that every wish you wished would come true.'

Kitty clapped her hands. 'Of course! And then you could wish for lots of chocolate, and a new bike, and a holiday on a liner, and a big art set, and all the books you ever wanted to read, and roast chicken every day, and lots of presents for Mum and Dad . . .'

'You'd get bored with it,' said Dan.

'What? Wishes coming true?' asked Kitty.

'No – roast chicken every day!' said Dan.

Kitty licked her lips. 'I wouldn't,' she said, 'I'd wish for roast chicken and roast potatoes and peas and loads of gravy and chocolate flakes and strawberry ice-cream and tangerines – and I'd have it all for breakfast, if I wanted!'

'Yuk,' said Daniel.

'So what would you wish for?' asked Kitty.

Daniel frowned and thought. Then he said, 'I know – I'd wish Dad could find a good job.'

Then Kitty felt a bit silly. 'Oh, so would I,' she said. 'But if every wish we wished came true we could have that AND all the other lovely things, couldn't we?'

'Yes, but I'd rather Dad had a job than your stupid old roast chicken,' said Daniel.

Kitty was quiet for a bit, then she got up and took out two

I wish!

candles. She set them in the candlesticks, put them in the middle of the table, then picked up the matches. She knew this was NOT allowed, so she had to be very quick. In a minute the candles were lit, and Kitty closed her eyes tightly.

'I wish . . . I wish . . . I wish . . . my wish would come true . . . I wish . . . I wish . . .'

'Kitty! What on earth are you doing with those candles?' said Mum, coming in through the back door with the washing basket. Just at that minute, Kitty blew the candles out.

'I'm making a wish,' said Kitty.

'I've told you NEVER to touch matches!' said Mum crossly.

'But Mum, this was really important. You know how you make a wish when you blow out your birthday candles? Well, I thought it might work even if it wasn't a birthday – if the wish was important enough.'

Mum sat down. She saw Kitty was being serious, so she asked, 'And what was your important wish, Kitty-Kat?'

'I can't tell you. It won't work if I tell you, will it? Oh Mum! I WISH wishes came true!'

'So do I, my love!' smiled Mum. 'But if all wishes came true, then I suppose we'd

I wish!

be living in fairyland. And I can't see you as a fairy, Kit!'

'I'd even put up with being a silly old fairy, if I could make my wish come true,' said Kitty.

About two hours later, she and Daniel were watching television in the sitting-room, when there was a loud bang, like the back door crashing open, then a shout, then a squeal – all from the kitchen.

'What's happening?' said Dan.

'Burglars!' whispered Kitty.

They both jumped up, ran to the kitchen – and saw Mum and Dad dancing, laughing, and knocking things over as they whirled round the small room.

'I've got that job, kids! The one I really wanted – down at the Civic Centre!' Dad yelled. 'I just called in and they told me!'

'It's so great! I'm so happy,' squealed Mum.

They held out their arms and Daniel and Kitty joined them in a massive family hug. Kitty felt she wanted to laugh and to cry, all at once.

The two candles were still on the table, and Kitty took one in each hand, waving them about.

'I told you! I told you!' she shouted.

'What?' asked Dad.

'I told Mum that my wish was an important one. I wished you'd get a job, Dad – and now you have!'

'So wishes do come true!' laughed Mum. 'You must be a fairy after all.'

'Well, in that case,' said Dan, 'can we have roast chicken tonight – just to prove it?'

And it was the best celebration supper Kitty had ever had.

I wish!

... I was grown up!

Kitty was fed up with being little. Every day she had to get up, find her school clothes, wash her face, clean her teeth, eat breakfast (and even if she didn't want it, Mum made her eat something) and go to school. Then Kitty had to learn things all day until it was time to come home, eat, wash, clean her teeth, and go to bed – even if she wasn't tired. Then it all started over again.

Kitty and friends

It was boring, she decided.

Very boring.

Always having to do things.

She looked at Mum and Dad and decided that they had a much nicer time. They both loved their jobs. They could buy things if they wanted to. They could watch television when they chose, and eat a biscuit when they felt like it, and go to bed the moment they felt tired, and not before.

It wasn't fair.

'I wish I was grown up,' said Kitty.

'Why?' asked Dad.

I wish!

'Because you can do what you like,' said Kitty.

'Don't you believe it!' said Dad.

One Saturday, Kitty woke to find that it was raining both inside and outside the house. Rain ran down the windows, and the sky was grey. But worse, Mum and Dad were getting cross with each other downstairs, and Kitty wanted to roll over and hide her head in the pillows.

But she got up, put on her dressing gown, and crept downstairs. She stopped outside the kitchen door, and listened.

'You were supposed to buy eggs,' said Mum.

'You know I'm working late. I thought you were glad I got this job!' said Dad.

'I can't cope with all the shopping, as well as work!' said Mum.

'I thought you'd paid the gas bill, but you haven't!' said Dad.

'You said you'd done it!'

'I didn't,' said Dad.

'Yes, you did!'

'It's your job!'

'Everything seems to be my job!' said Mum.

'Here we go again!' said Dad.

'There's always so much to think about,' sighed Mum.

'I know!' said Dad.

'I never have any time for myself,' said Mum.

'Who does?' said Dad, crossly.

Kitty put her head round the door. 'Can I have some breakfast?' she asked. Mum and Dad looked at her. They

I wish!

both looked cross and worried. Suddenly Kitty decided that it must be *awful* to be grown up!

'Shall we play a game?' she asked.

'No,' said Mum.

'Why not?' asked Kitty.

'Because I don't want to!' said Mum.

'You sound just like me, Mum!' said Kitty. 'Maybe you're still a little girl, after all.'

'Oh, I wish I was,' said Mum, in a gloomy voice, picking up a cloth to clean the sink.

Dad looked at Kitty and Kitty looked at Dad, and the idea must have hit them both at the same time. Dad took the cloth out of Mum's hand, and Kitty took hold of her and started pulling her towards the door.

'Where are we going?' asked Mum.

'To play!' said Kitty.

It was the best morning they had had for a long, long time. As the rain pattered on the windows, they got all the old games

out of the cupboard, and found the dice, and began to play. *Ludo. Snakes and Ladders. Draughts. Snap.* When Dan came downstairs they started *Monopoly* – and Mum started to scream with excitement as her piles of money grew, and she bought lots of houses and hotels.

'I'm winning – you haven't got a chance!' she laughed.

'This is better than TV,' said Daniel.

'Better than work!' said Dad.

I wish!

'Let's play the detective game next!' said Kitty.

'No, I think we should play *Happy Families*,' said Dad, reaching across and giving Mum a little pat on the head.

'All right,' said Mum happily.

'You know something?' said Kitty. 'I wish I didn't have to grow up. I wish I could stay just like I am forever.'

'That wish will probably come true, knowing you!' laughed Dad.

I wish!

... it was always Christmas!

Kitty woke early. Her room was dark. She stretched her toes down to the bottom of the bed and . . . YES! She felt something heavy, and bulky, that rustled a bit when she moved her feet. It could only be – a stocking!

At last it was Christmas Day, after all the weeks of waiting. Kitty's tummy gave a dip and a swoop – like a rollercoaster. Then she sat up, put on her light, and reached forward to grab her stocking. As she pulled it up the bed, little packages spilled out of the top.

Oh . . . Father Christmas had been extra kind this year!

Her tummy went up and down again, so she had to take a deep breath. The she started to tear the wrappings off the little parcels, squeaking loudly as she saw each present.

There was a rubber shaped like a pair of sunglasses, and a pencil-sharpener shaped

like a car, and two wooden puzzles, and some joke blood, and a chocolate mouse, and some Dracula teeth, and a notebook with PRIVATE written on it, and a set of crayons and . . . so many things!

Kitty went on and on, until her floor was covered with scraps of paper, and she had reached the bottom.

There she found the usual satsuma – and beneath that, in the toe, the potato which said she had been naughty at least once.

Actually Kitty thought Father Christmas was pretty good, because she could easily have got a whole stocking full of potatoes, enough for plates and plates of chips!

She stuck the Dracula teeth in her mouth and ran into Daniel's room, yelling, 'GRRRRRRRRR!'

He had already smeared his joke blood all over his face. So after Kitty had looked at his stocking presents for a couple of minutes, the two of them rushed into Mum and Dad's room, making spooky noises. They knew Mum and Dad would turn over and mumble, 'It's too early.' Just like they always did.

That was one of the lovely things about Christmas. It was always the same, year after year.

They always went downstairs together, and had breakfast, and then went to peep at the big presents under the tree in the sitting-room. But they weren't allowed to open them until after church.

Kitty and friends

Mum always liked them all to go to church together on Christmas Day. To tell the truth, they didn't go much the rest of the year! But Mum said Christmas was about Jesus being born, not just presents, and anyway she loved singing carols.

Kitty and Dad didn't mind because the church was decorated with holly and tinsel, and the vicar was very jolly and funny, and little children took their toys to play with, and everybody looked happy.

After church they went home quickly, and gave each other their main presents. This year, Kitty had a watch with a red strap. She was so pleased – because it felt very grown up. Mum gave Dad a new jacket, and Dad gave Mum a necklace with matching earrings, and Dan got a computer game – and there were lots of other things too.

Kitty was very proud of the presents she gave. She'd made Mum and Dad a

I wish!

calendar, which they loved. But she had saved up to buy them a little plate as well. Best of all, she had bought Daniel a geometry set, which he needed for school – and he was really surprised!

Then Dad went to get Gran, and before lunch she gave them all her knitted presents – which were a bit funny and the wrong size, but it didn't matter because Gran had worked so hard with her needles.

The house was filled with the smell of roast turkey, and at last they sat down to a huge lunch. It was lovely! They pulled their crackers and sat wearing their silly hats and reading the jokes and swapping the little cracker toys.

As it started to go dark, Mum brought in the Christmas pudding, and the blue flames lit up her face.

'Everybody make their own wish!' she called.

Much later, when they had played games, and Gran had gone upstairs for a rest, and the house felt all warm and sleepy, Kitty started to feel sad.

It was dark outside. Soon it would be time for supper, and then Christmas Day would be over for another year.

'What's the matter, Kitty?' asked Dad.

'Nothing,' said Kitty.

'Yes, there is. I can see by your face. Come up here and tell me about it!'

I wish!

Kitty climbed on his knee, snuggled down against his jumper, and sighed. 'Oh Dad, it's not fair! I wish it could always be Christmas!'

'So that's it!'

'It's so boring when Christmas is over!' Kitty moaned.

'No, it's not!' said Dad. 'Tomorrow we're going next door to have supper with

William's family, and we'll play lots of games. Then you'll go to school and be able to show off your new watch to everyone.'

Kitty looked at her wrist and smiled. She *loved* her watch! It was fun to tell everyone the time . . .

'Then you'll have your birthday, and then it'll be Easter and you'll have a chocolate egg – or maybe two! And what comes after that?'

'Summer,' said Kitty.

'Yes – and you like going to the swimming baths, and eating ice-cream, and we'll probably have a week away by the sea, now we can afford it. If it was always Christmas there'd be nothing to look forward to!'

Kitty sat up. 'Yes, and think of all the presents I'd have to buy. That would be awful!'

'Oh, Kitty! You're so bad!' laughed Dad.